THOMAS & FRIENDS™

Edward the Hero

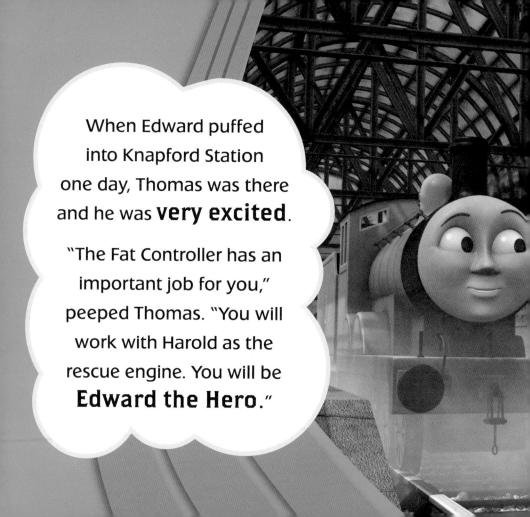

When Edward puffed into Knapford Station one day, Thomas was there and he was **very excited**.

"The Fat Controller has an important job for you," peeped Thomas. "You will work with Harold as the rescue engine. You will be **Edward the Hero**."

Edward thought that he would like to be a hero. But he was worried. He wasn't sure he'd be very good at it. In fact, he didn't have any idea **how** to be a hero.

KNAPFORD

Just then, Gordon **raced** and **roared** through the station, pushing Rocky. Gordon was strong and fast and stern.

"Gordon is a hero," thought Edward. "I must be more like him." And he puffed out of the station.

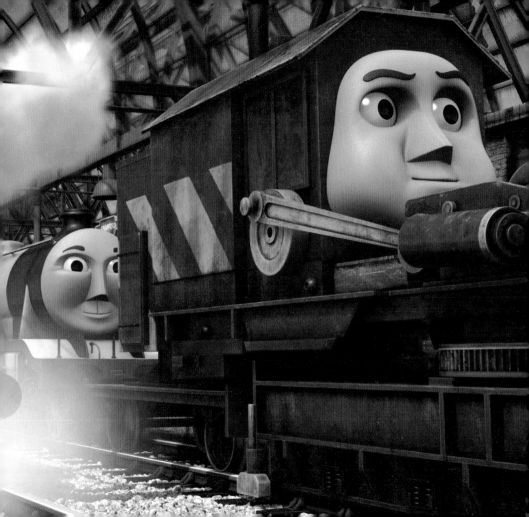

But as Edward puffed along trying to be strong and fast and stern, he saw Charlie looking sad. Charlie had forgotten all the jokes he wanted to tell the children.

So Edward told Charlie some more jokes, and made him **giggle** and *jiggle!*

"You're *funny!*" chuffed Charlie.

That made Edward happy. But then he remembered something …

"Oh dear," he sighed "I wasn't strong, fast or stern. I was just **funny**. I must try harder to be a hero."

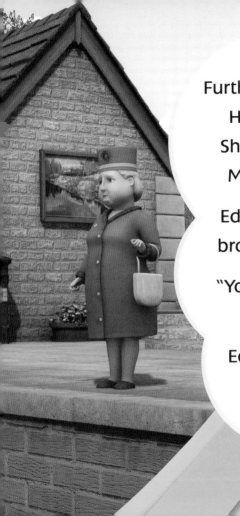

Further along the line, Dowager Hatt was looking worried. She had sent her suitcase to Maron Station by mistake.

Edward raced to fetch it and brought it safely back to her.

"You are very kind," she said.

"Just **kind**?" sighed Edward. "I must try harder to be a hero."

But just then, Edward saw Farmer McColl's dog. He was lost, and scared of the engine.

Very **gently**, Edward edged closer. The dog jumped aboard and Edward took him back to Farmer McColl.

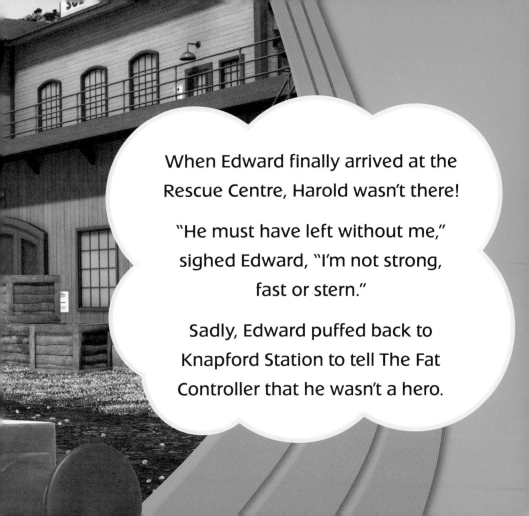

When Edward finally arrived at the Rescue Centre, Harold wasn't there!

"He must have left without me," sighed Edward, "I'm not strong, fast or stern."

Sadly, Edward puffed back to Knapford Station to tell The Fat Controller that he wasn't a hero.

But on the way he passed Farmer McColl
and a little later he passed Charlie.
They both called out the same thing:

"There he is! **Edward the Hero!**"

Edward didn't understand.

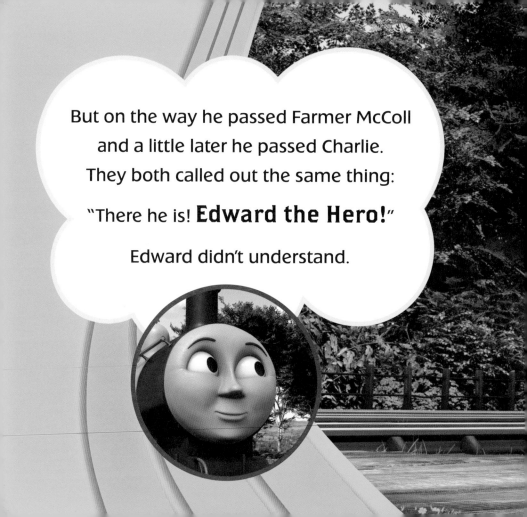

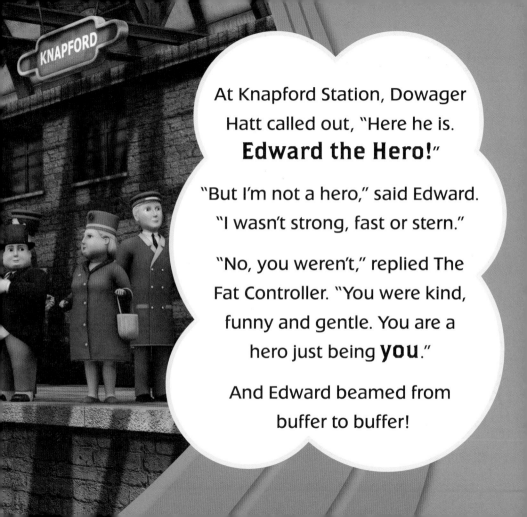

At Knapford Station, Dowager Hatt called out, "Here he is. **Edward the Hero!**"

"But I'm not a hero," said Edward. "I wasn't strong, fast or stern."

"No, you weren't," replied The Fat Controller. "You were kind, funny and gentle. You are a hero just being **you**."

And Edward beamed from buffer to buffer!

PEEP! PEEP!

The End